THE

# PULL *of the* OCEAN

THE

PULL *of the* OCEAN

JEAN-CLAUDE MOURLEVAT

translated from the French by Y. Maudet

DELACORTE PRESS

Published by Delacorte Press
an imprint of Random House Children's Books
a division of Random House, Inc.
New York

Originally published in France in 1999 under the title *L'enfant Océan*
by Editions Pocket Jeunesse
All rights reserved.

www.randomhouse.com/teens

Educators and librarians, for a variety of teaching tools,
visit us at www.randomhouse.com/teachers

Library of Congress Cataloging-in-Publication Data
Mourlevat, Jean-Claude.
[Enfant océan. English]
The pull of the ocean / Jean-Claude Mourlevat ; translated from the French by Y. Maudet.
p. cm.
Summary: Loosely based on Charles Perrault's "Tom Thumb," seven brothers in modern-
day France flee their poor parents' farm, led by the youngest who, although mute and
unusually small, is exceptionally wise.
ISBN-13: 978-0-385-73348-9 (trade) – ISBN-13: 978-0-385-90364-6 (glb)
ISBN-10: 0-385-73348-8 (trade) – ISBN-10: 0-385-90364-2 (glb)
[1. Size–Fiction. 2. Twins–Fiction. 3. Brothers–Fiction. 4. Mutism, Elective–Fiction.
5. France–Fiction.] I. Maudet, Y. II. Tom Thumb. English. III. Title.
PZ7.M8646Pu 2006
[Fic]–dc22                                    2006001802

The text of this book is set in 12-point Goudy.

Printed in the United States of America

10 9 8 7 6 5 4 3 2

First Edition

THE

PULL *of the* OCEAN

For Emma

# PART ONE

The youngest one looked
very fragile and uttered not a word.
—"Tom Thumb," Charles Perrault

# one

ACCOUNT OF NATHALIE JOSSE,
THIRTY-TWO YEARS OLD, SOCIAL WORKER

I'm one of the last people who saw Yann Doutreleau alive. At least, I believe I am. He was settled next to me in the car. I say settled rather than seated, because his short legs lay flat on the seat, straight as sticks, his feet pointing toward the glove compartment. The safety belt hung loosely around his chest. I could have put him in the car seat at the back, but I didn't dare. He looked too much like a large doll. This happened last November. Do you remember that rainy week at the beginning of the month? What miserable weather! It rained cats and dogs when I took Yann home that morning. I never saw him again.

My windshield wipers are about as efficient as drumsticks and I was driving at no more than twenty miles per hour on the county road. Had I known it would be the last time I'd see Yann, I would have looked at him more closely. Now it's too late.

I can still remember him, wedged deep in the seat, resolute, fiddling with his hands, his funny little baby hands, red and plump. Dressed in a suit jacket and gray cotton pants, he seemed to have come from another century. Who would dare dress a child this way, if not to humiliate him? They had to be clothes from the attic. My throat tightens up when I think of it.

I had never seen a little boy like him before. What was his height? Two feet? Two feet and a half? In any case, he was hardly as tall as a two-year-old child. Yet he was ten. Yann was a miniature.

"Sweet," "cute," "charming," "adorable": that's what you felt like saying about him, except that an old, knowing expression around his eyes and mouth kept you from doing so. He had none of the deformities that you find in dwarfs. Everything about him was harmonious, but everything was . . . small.

It was pouring. Wind gusted. The map unfolded loosely on my knees. It couldn't be much farther away. A few hundred yards, perhaps. I had probably missed the path, gone past without noticing it. Everything was possible in that rain. I made a U-turn and tried to concentrate. It was all the more irritating that Yann knew the way. But he wasn't cooperating.

"Is it in this direction? Right or left?" I asked at the beginning. "If you don't want to talk, at least point the way with your finger."

I might as well have questioned my umbrella.

I still knew almost nothing about my little passenger. Only that he was ten years old, that his name was Yann, and that he was mute. He had arrived at school that morning, looking dazed, and without his book bag. When questioned, his brothers had not been very talkative.

"It's the father threw it swimming," one of them had finally said before snuffling up a one-inch booger.

Translation: the father had thrown the book bag in a well, or in a pond, or in some body of water.

I'd encountered some crazy cases in my maddening profession, but this one was a first. I looked at

4

the child surreptitiously, at the thick shoes gaping at the soles, at the frayed pants, at the sleeves of a brown sweater that were too long for the jacket's. My throat tightened. I was about to pat Yann's knee and tell him "Don't worry, it will be all right," when the path appeared suddenly on our right. A small panel, half hidden in the weeds, spelled out: Perrault's.

———————————————

I parked the car at the entrance of the courtyard and waited before getting out. The rain was pouring in buckets.

"Is this it?" I asked.

Without looking at me, the child nodded slightly. It was here.

The farm was ugly and dirty. A huge heap of scrap iron was piled in the yard. Weeds were growing on top of it. Near the door of a shed, whose roof was falling apart, a large, skinny dog was barking.

The Doutreleaus were well known at school. The father had a farm. Yann was the seventh child. The six others were all twins. The two older boys were fourteen, the next thirteen, the youngest eleven. Each year, or almost each year, in September, the sixth-grade teachers witnessed the latest delivery of Doutreleaus. All the twins were tall for their age, but skinny, probably due to undernourishment. And none showed any aptitude for school.

Yann came last and alone. Like the period at the end of a sentence.

The dog barked more loudly near the shed. A

door opened farther down and a woman planted herself on the threshold. Her apron was filthy, and a frying pan hung from one of her arms.

"Is that your mother?"

Silence. I got out of the car, opened my umbrella and helped Yann out. Together we waded across the courtyard toward the motionless woman. The mud came up to our ankles.

"Hello. My name is Nathalie Josse. I'm a social worker. I'd like to . . ."

The dog had sneaked up behind me, and I had the impression that it was waiting for the right moment to pounce and tear off a piece of my calf. As a reflex, I took the child's hand in mine. His head hung low, and I shuddered because his tiny hand was as rough as a lumberjack's or a construction worker's.

It didn't occur to the woman to quiet the dog or to come forward to meet us. Neither did she seem surprised to see her son come home at this time of day or accompanied. She simply watched us with the vacant look of a fish and waited for things to unfold.

"Are you Mrs. Doutreleau?" I tried again. "My name is Nathalie—"

"What's he done?" Her tone was dry and threatening.

"Yann hasn't done anything. I just wanted—"

The frying pan went flying, grazing my shoulder before landing full blast on the dog's head. He whimpered pitifully as he ran to take refuge behind the house.

"Whaddya want, then?"

"Well, I'm bringing Yann back because he came

to school without his book bag and he didn't look well. Could I talk to you about it?"

"See the father."

Even with the umbrella, the rain was running down our heads, flooding my face, icing my shoulders. I insisted and the woman repeated:

"See the father."

Seeing that she wasn't budging from the doorway, and that she gave me a hard look, I understood that she wasn't about to let me in. So after the third "See the father," I gave up.

"And when can I see him?"

"Tomorrow."

"In the morning?"

Instead of answering me, she addressed the child for the first time.

"Get in here, you!"

Yann let go of my hand and slipped into the small space between his mother and the door. Before he disappeared, he did something strange. Without turning his body, he swiveled his head and looked at me over his shoulder. This didn't last more than three seconds, yet the image is imprinted on my mind more clearly than any photograph. Ever since, I keep seeing his face, his eyes firmly locked onto mine. I had the uneasy feeling that he was talking to me. And yet he didn't say a word. He didn't move. At first, I read reproach in his eyes.

*Congratulations, some fine work you've done.*

But right after, I read some gratitude.

*You've been nice to me. You couldn't have known.*

I try to convince myself that this is all there was to his look back, but I know now that his eyes were telling me something else. Were shouting something else. And what they were shouting was *Help me!*

I didn't understand or didn't want to understand. I told myself that I would take care of things later, that it was one of those situations that could wait until the next day. But there was no next day.

# two

ACCOUNT OF MARTHE DOUTRELEAU,
FORTY YEARS OLD, YANN'S MOTHER

What was that city girl thinking? That we was gonna have tea in the parlor? That we was gonna nibble some cookies? Comin' over without warning, shaking her behind and wanting to teach me a lesson! If only stupid Corniaud had torn out a piece of her calf, but all he done is bark that yapper. I ended up sending the frying pan on his nose to make him shut his trap. I nearly caught the girl; too bad I didn't. "He didn't look well!" she says, that bitch.

Not well! Poor little darling! He hasn't looked well in ten years. He does that to piss us off, to make life impossible for us. What they all got to pity him for, that one? 'Cause he's a midget? If he behaved like the others, we'd treat him like the rest, midget or not. But he has to pretend, to put on airs, with his know-it-all, too-good-to-say-nothing looks he gives you. He's got a tongue, ain't he? I made him whole just like his brothers. So why's he bent on saying nothing? What does he blame us for, tell me? I delivered him into the world same as the others. Is it my fault if he came alone? And that he's the size of a fist? His brothers came in pairs and weighed a good eight pounds each. But I didn't even feel this one pop out. It was just like laying an egg.

We kept him anyhow. We thought his size might come in handy for certain chores. Like entering places where others couldn't fit. Or to sort small things. What'd we know? Nature screwed us, but maybe nature would reward us in the end. So we waited. Besides, he was cheap to feed.

Well, for a disappointment, it was a disappointment. He acts like he's a genius. Guess it's understandable: you don't get worn out being a know-it-all and you get fewer blisters on your hands. It started when he was about five, when we sent him to school. His brothers were already attending school, but at least they didn't try to learn nothin'. But him, he loved it, and not just a little. He made a point of showing it too. Probably his way to tell us that we were morons. We put up with his superior attitude way too long, him with his nose in his notebook, his tongue hanging out while he wrote things out all neat and such. That sure changed the day he gave his father backtalk. It was hay time. He must have been seven or eight, I can't remember no more, 'cause I don't keep track. In any case, he wasn't taller than the year before, of that I'm sure. There are even times when I wonder whether he wasn't actually shrinking. But I had better things to do than measure him. So like I said, it was hay time and he was supposed to help rake at the back. That wasn't asking for the moon, right? Well, he didn't move his ass, just showed us his notebook as if to say, "I ain't going. I've work to do." Yeah, like he really had better things to take care of, right?

Doutreleau didn't like that. Not one bit. He saw red. He smacked him a good one across the nose. It even bled. He has a heavy hand, Doutreleau does; I told him so a hundred times. One of these days he's gonna knock out one of them kids for good and who'll be left explaining things to the police? Not him, that's for sure. He'll hide just like he did when that girl showed up. He's not talkative. When people drop by he takes off and leaves me alone to deal. Me, I've got a quick hand. Not heavy, just quick. It takes off swiftly and does the job. In my opinion, that's good enough. No need to daze 'em. All the same, after getting smacked, that Yann, he walked a straight line. When asked to do something, he did it, and usually twice instead of once. Except that he started to look at us with that smarmy expression of his. He'd make you look away, that little snake. You've gotta hit him to make him stop. Who does he think he is?

Well, it was tolerable until then. But now he's in sixth grade. And he brings back praises from school! How do they know he's even intelligent, considering he don't say a word? Did they open his brain or something? So, of course, he thinks he's the pope, puffing out his chest and looking at us from on high, that little shrimp. Isn't that the top?

I was expecting the girl. I knew they'd come, her or someone else, since Doutreleau had thrown the shrimp's book bag in the water. He goes too far, Doutreleau does, but you've gotta understand. Four times we called the brat to come eat his soup. But no, he stood by the window, his nose in his book; the midget wouldn't budge. So Doutreleau gets up suddenly. This time he didn't hit. He gets up, calm like he was gonna take a leak, and puts the notebook, the book, all the gear in the schoolbag, and as cool as John the Baptist, without shouting or nothing, out he went. We saw him walk toward the well and we heard a plop and that was that. He came back and finished his soup. The brat didn't move. He let everything happen. He kept looking at the table, where the book had been and no longer was, and then he went straight up to bed, as if nothing had happened.

When he passed by me, I asked him if he wanted a piece of bread considering he hadn't eaten his soup. Whatever you say, a mother is a mother. But he walked by without looking up, just as if I had been Corniaud barking at him. Try to be good, huh! I learned my lesson!

# three

ACCOUNT OF LOUIS DOUTRELEAU,
FORTY-ONE YEARS OLD, YANN'S FATHER

As long as we have a piece of stale bread to soak in water, the Marthe'll call it soup. And when there's none left, she'll make herself look pitiful and beg for help at the office of social services. When there's nothin' more to get from them, she'll stand at the church door on Sundays, her hand extended. Without shame. She'll keep her head down and avert her eyes. Women are like that. They're like animals. They'll do anything when their little ones are starving. They grow teeth as long as wolves' and put up with any humiliation.

Not me.

I'd rather croak. I'll never ask no one for nothin'. And my boys'll never ask for nothin' either.

# four

ACCOUNT FROM FABIEN DOUTRELEAU,
FOURTEEN YEARS OLD, YANN'S BROTHER

In the middle of the night, I felt something move next to me. It was Yann. He got up, which made the bed creak. He wasn't going to pee, since we aren't allowed to in the middle of the night. We all pee before going to bed. We line up in the yard near the outhouse, and when the father isn't looking, we have fun aiming as far as we can. In winter, it's easy to measure 'cause the pee leaves traces in the snow.

It makes us laugh. Then we go up to our room until the next morning.

So like I said, Yann got up. I asked him where he was going and he told me that our parents were having a fight. He was going downstairs to listen and said he'd be back right away. He didn't actually *say* any of this. He made me understand. 'Cause Yann says things in signs. He doesn't say a word. He just mimics, which is worth a thousand words. He goes at supersonic speed. If we try to imitate him, it takes forever and we never get anywhere. But with him, it's quick and crystal clear. He hardly even moves, just a bit in the face and fingers.

For a long time, I thought Rémy and me, the older brothers, were the only ones who understood Yann, 'cause we're used to him, and he likes us. But that's not the case. Anyone can understand Yann. All it takes is for him to decide to talk to you. You have to gain his confidence. Period. For instance, he's never said anything to the father or the mother. He doesn't even look at them. Among the brothers, he talks to Rémy and me the most. Maybe 'cause we've been sharing the same bed for ten years.

There are three beds in the room upstairs. One nearest to the stairs, for the youngest twins, one in the middle of the room, for the middle twins, and one at the back, under the window, for Rémy and me. In our home, the older you become, the more you get pushed near the window, which takes you farther away from the stairs and the parents sleeping downstairs. Not a bad thing: you get farther away from the blows at the same time.

When Yann was born, he was so small, they added him to our bed. And there he stayed. That's the way it happened. When he was a baby, Rémy and me took care of him. The mother didn't come up. When he teethed and cried too much, we melted some sugar in water, dipped our little finger in it and made him suck on it. The parents took a dislike to him. We don't know why. Maybe 'cause he's different. Or 'cause he doesn't do any work but eats all the same. They go too far. A piece of bread and half a potato and Yann is full. A sparrow eats more than he does. Also, they're afraid of him, I think. He wasn't even four years old when he made them turn away just by looking at them. The mother can't stand it; she clouts him. So now he doesn't look at them at all. Yann can see the difference between Rémy and me. He's the only one who does. He never fails. From far or close, back or front, nighttime or daytime, whatever the circumstance, for Yann, Rémy is Rémy and I'm me. We look as alike as one egg to another egg, but Yann never gets it wrong. Sometimes I think he's weird. Not 'cause of his height, but 'cause of the way he makes himself understood so quickly and so easily. Sometimes he tells me something complicated and afterward I realize that he hasn't even batted an eyelash. He's just looked at me. Some people would be frightened by that. Not me.

But let's come back to that famous night. After five minutes at most, I had nearly fallen asleep again when Yann returned and tugged at the sleeve of my sweater (we sleep with our woolens 'cause it's cold). I opened my eyes and I saw him planted in front of my nose. It was the first time I saw him panicked. So, right away, I knew it was serious. His face and small hands started to move in the glimmer of the candle. The more he talked, the more panicked I became.

*We have to go, Fabien,* he said. *All of us! Quickly! Before dawn!*

I was about to ask why but got scared. Too scared to want to hear the answer. Besides, I think I already knew.

"But Yann, it's pouring . . . it's pitch dark," I mumbled.

*That's precisely why,* he said. *The rain is making so much noise, they won't hear us leave. We can't wait. We have to hurry and go now. Quick. Because they want to . . . they are going to . . .*

He didn't want to say the word. The word was *kill,* of course. But either he was unable to spit it out or he didn't want to.

*They want to harm us*, he ended up saying. *Do you understand?*

When I think that he was ten years old and me fourteen . . . you would have thought it was the other way around. He was trying hard to spare me. But I still started to cry. The idea of running away in the dark of night, under the pouring rain with my brothers, seemed awful to me. Then Yann did something gentle and tender. He stroked my head and my cheeks with his two little hands.

*Don't be afraid*, it meant. *I'll take care of each of you. Don't lose courage.*

I got up, got dressed, and both of us woke our brothers, going from one to the other. As soon as they opened an eye, I explained to them what I knew and what to do. If I had been alone, they wouldn't have believed me, but with Yann it was easier.

"Okay, okay, I'm coming," they each said.

That night, Yann became our leader. It just happened.

We dressed as warmly as we could and went downstairs. The steps creaked badly, but the patter of the rain was so loud and the wind so strong, the parents heard nothing. The clock in the kitchen said two o'clock on the dot.

We crossed the courtyard. Corniaud didn't flinch. We walked straight ahead along the path, then onto the road. In a few seconds, we were drenched, freezing . . . and lost.

Yann walked in front of us. I followed closely behind with Rémy. Our brothers brought up the rear, holding hands. The youngest ones were whining.

# five

ACCOUNT OF DANIEL SANZ,
FORTY-EIGHT YEARS OLD, TRUCK DRIVER

All of a sudden, a tribe of kids appeared in my head-lights. They flailed their arms in the air.

"Stop! Stop!"

You should have seen them all with their mouths wide open. You didn't have to be a lip-reader to guess what they wanted: to come aboard my truck.

I didn't have to brake much. The road is bad in that area and it was worse with the rain. On top of it, I was coming out of a sharp turn. So I was going nearly at crawling speed. I opened the passenger door and in they climbed. I counted one, two, three, four—all soaked to the bone and dripping wet. Plus two more! They looked alike. And they shivered so badly, their teeth were chattering. I thought I had seen the end of the procession.

"Make sure you close the door!" I shouted to the last one.

But he turned back, went down a step, and extended his arms. Up he came again with something in his hands—something that looked like a baby.

I was stunned! Totally stunned!

"And where are you going?" I asked.

No answer. The tallest one sat beside me and vaguely pointed in front, meaning "somewhere ahead."

I laughed. "Where do you live?"

Somewhere ahead! Everything was "somewhere

ahead" with them! *Well, we'll see*, I told myself. There were blankets in the rear. I pulled out two of them.

"Throw these on your backs!" I said.

They began to shed half their clothes. Off went the sweaters and shirts, and they rolled themselves up in the blankets. The cab was a mess! They looked like a litter of kittens in a basket.

"The smaller ones could go in the back," I said.

No sooner said than done. They climbed on top of each other. They trampled over each other. All this without a peep of laughter. This struck me because when kids climb into the back of the cab, they usually giggle. Only the two older ones stayed in front, with the smaller boy between them.

"How old is the little guy?" I asked.

No answer.

"Where do you come from? Did you run away?"

Silence. Their story sure wasn't clear.

My first thought was to leave them at the village police station. But I didn't know where the police station was and I would've had to turn around. Have you ever made a U-turn in a thirty-five-ton truck? Instead I headed to Périgueux. It's a town about fifty miles away, a one-hour drive at most, and I could drop them off there. I was wrong to do that, I know it now, but it's easy to be wise after the fact. Those who do nothing make no mistake.

During the time it took me to sort the whole thing out, to weigh the pros and cons, they had all fallen asleep. Life is strange, don't tell me it's not. Fifteen minutes before, I had been alone in my truck, listening to the radio. Suddenly we were eight in there. Seven of us were sleeping, and I was laughing. What made the situation even stranger was that before I picked them up, I was thinking about my own kids. The kids Catherine and I *can't* have. It takes its toll on me because I love kids. If we had only one, nobody would be happier than us. Sometimes I imagine myself cuddling with and babbling to this child. When I realize that I'm talking to myself in the truck, it makes me sad.

Then in the dark of night, this brood of kids fell from the sky like lost kittens. *Poor kids*, I told myself, feeling sorry for them. They were wearing weird clothes. Definitely not Lacoste, I guarantee you.

A little before reaching Périgueux, there is a village with a police station right by the highway. You can't miss it. I pulled up to the parking lot not far away, didn't shut off the motor, and got out without closing the door. Taking one last look at the kids, I walked to the building. I swear to you they were all sleeping like logs when I left, or else they were faking it really well. I reached the police station and rang the bell once or twice. A light went on on the second floor, and thirty seconds later a policeman in pajamas opened the window and asked me what I wanted. Without raising my voice much, I explained to him that there was a whole litter of funny little cats in my truck and that it would be wise for him to take a look. He said he'd be right down. I lit a cigarette while I waited for him. The rain was easing now. He came down finally and we walked toward the truck.

Well, not much suspense there, right? Easy to guess. When I opened the door to show the policeman my catch, I looked like a dope. There was no one on board. No one, I'm telling you. Gone. All of them. Not even a forgotten sock, nothing. Only the two blankets piled up on the passenger seat.

We looked around with my flashlight. Nothing. So I turned off the ignition and went to give a statement. When I was done, it was close to three-thirty in the morning. Where had they come from? Where were they going, these kids? I wondered whether they really existed, or if I had dreamed the whole thing. I hit the road again. After a while, for my own benefit, I said loudly, "Good luck, kiddos," and tried to think about something else.

# six

ACCOUNT OF RÉMY DOUTRELEAU,
FOURTEEN YEARS OLD, YANN'S BROTHER

We took off our wet clothes and wrapped ourselves in the blankets. Yann nestled himself between Fabien and me and closed his eyes. But I know him well and I was sure he wasn't sleeping. The little ones piled up in the back behind us. The driver asked us questions at the beginning: where we were going to, where we were coming from, stuff like that. I pointed ahead vaguely. He seemed satisfied with that answer. In any case, he stopped asking anything.

It was cozy inside. The motor was running smoothly, warmly. The road went by in the headlights, very dark in the rain, the leafless trees pointing their skinny limbs toward the sky. We crossed a village now and then, followed by a stretch of flat land. I wished we could stay in that truck forever, that it would go nonstop till the end of the night, till the ocean. 'Cause I was sure we were going west. We were going to the place Yann had shown to us with his finger, one summer night.

*Over there is west*, he had said. *The sky is bigger than here, and then comes the ocean.* He pointed through the little window of our room.

The ocean. We wondered how he knew where it was, since he was barely four years old at the time and no one had told him about it. But already, nothing he said surprised us. We believed him totally and when we looked out the window, we no longer saw old neighbor Colle's meadow, with its apple trees, fence, and pond. We looked intensely at the gray horizon and saw the sky expand. We saw the ocean. We could even hear its huge waves crashing on the beach.

That's why this truck, which was whisking us away in the magic of night, had to be going west. To enjoy the ride longer, I fought falling asleep. I imagined that this quiet man next to me was our father. That the pretty woman in the picture on the dashboard was our mother.

"Come on, guys, I'll take you for a ride," he would say.

She would complain, "But what about school tomorrow?"

And the seven of us would cry and beg until she gave in. Then we would be with him in the truck.

The others would all be sleeping, except me. 'Cause the oldest one doesn't go to sleep like a baby. He stays awake to keep his father company.

"You okay, my boy? You're not sleeping?"

"I'm okay," I would answer proudly.

'Cause fathers like this one, who travel through the night in their giant trucks, alone, fearless, when the whole world is asleep in the warmth of their homes, I say you can be proud to be their son.

But this sort of dream doesn't last long. The man next to me was not our father. Our father has no truck, only a tractor and an old car that won't start in winter. He kicks it with his dirty boots and shouts so loud that it frightens us.

What would happen when he put his hands on us again? I turned to Yann for courage, but Fabien's eyes met mine. He smiled, meaning: "We're okay, right?"

I smiled back and added a little grimace. It meant: "We're fine, but for how long?" Then I closed my eyes and fell asleep.

———

*We're all getting off. Quick! Quick!*

Yann was shaking us with all his strength, hitting us with his tiny hands and gathering our clothes. The truck had stopped but the engine was running. I saw the driver walking toward a building: the police station. In less than a minute we were all outside, half naked, holding our shoes against our stomachs. We ran toward the ditch and went over it as best we could.

*Run! Run!*

We ran. At full speed and straight ahead. The ground felt flat and soft under our feet. It had to be a soccer field. But it was awfully slippery. Max, one of the young twins, fell first. A first-rate crash. His feet went up as high as his head. Then Victor, his twin, hit the ground. Every five yards we went down in turn. I even think we did it on purpose at the end. Soaked for soaked, dirty for dirty, why not go all out? That's what we told ourselves. They say people pay for mud baths. Tepid mud, probably. This one was icy but it was free. When we reached the end of the field, Yann was missing. We turned and waited until he came in the night. He was trotting slowly. He doesn't know how to run, so Yann trots like a toddler. We were a little ashamed to have forgotten him. A few yards from us, he slipped and fell backward. It made a *splash* in the mud. We couldn't help laughing and he laughed with us.

At that point, I knew we would make it. In spite of the cold, in spite of the dark and the fear, in spite of everything, we would manage. I went toward him and took him in my arms.

Behind us were the wooden bleachers for the spectators. It was a stadium, all right. We went to hide under them, going to the darkest corner, where we huddled against each other. Gradually we got our breath back, but as we quieted down, we realized that our teeth were chattering. I knew that the cold would kill us if we stayed there.

# seven

ACCOUNT OF JEAN-MICHEL HEYCKEN,
FORTY-FOUR YEARS OLD, WRITER

François had warned me:

"You want a quiet spot? I've exactly what you need. Even better, it's the most beautiful house. It belonged to my great-great-aunt, who died six months ago. You're not afraid of ghosts, are you? Fine. Then I'll describe the layout: from the dining room—a little heavy on the decoration, though you might enjoy it if you like prevailing brown tones—you'll have an unrestricted view of the municipal stadium. Practice sessions are every Wednesday, matches every other Sunday. The Formica kitchen overlooks the next houses. You're not prone to depression? Good. Now on to the bedroom: wallpaper depicts hunting scenes, with lots of pheasants, if I remember correctly. It even covers the ceiling. That's it! As for the phone, it's been disconnected, and there is no TV. Should you have any problems, the police station is only two hundred yards away. Sounds exciting, no? Lastly, since you stubbornly refuse to take your car, you should know that the nearest movie theater is about thirty miles away. You can take one of two buses to get there. The first one departs at six-thirty in the morning. Still want to go?"

Sure, I wanted to go. More than ever. This house, lost somewhere in the depths of the

Dordogne, seemed to me like paradise on earth. The ideal spot, where I would at last be able to write. Write in the morning, in the evening, at night, without ever being disturbed. Write until my eyes and my back ached. I thanked François and two days later I was on the train to Limoges, as excited as a child going to the seaside for the first time. To crown my good fortune, this was at the beginning of November. Everyone was complaining about the cold and rain we'd had for weeks. Except for me, since I dislike the heat. Or the sun. It burns the eyes and renders you useless. It definitely keeps me from working. I should have been born in Iceland or Latvia, one of those countries where night comes at four o'clock in the afternoon, at least as I imagine it.

Well, as soon as I arrived at my little paradise, I

put my feet into the now departed great-aunt's slippers, set up my writing equipment on the dining room table and began to write.

On the night of November 7 to 8, I had been in the house for three days. It was about three in the morning. I had worked diligently until then and was treating myself to a little snack in the kitchen. Actually, it was more of a feast: some leftover chicken with mayonnaise and a beer. I was happy and relaxed, feeling that I'd achieved a lot. My novel was off to a good start. It was set during a summer heat wave, somewhere on the Normandy coast. A small-time supermarket thief falls in love with the girl at the cash register. The more I progressed with my story, the clearer I saw this petty thief and the more I liked him. At times I was moved to tears when writing.

I finished my feast, and as I crossed the dining

room to go to bed, I unintentionally looked out at the stadium below. At first, I wondered if I was half crazy: I thought I saw some disjointed puppets scampering across the lawn, falling every other step. I told myself that there were only two possibilities: either I was drunk after only one beer, or the local team had lost its twelfth match in a row the previous Sunday and had decided to hide its shame and train in the dark from now on.

I stuck my nose against the window and tried to see better. It looked as if the figures were disappearing under the bleachers. Totally weird! I pulled up a chair and waited for what would happen next. A truck was idling in the police station parking lot. The engine ran for a while, then stopped. The beam of a flashlight went around the truck, carefully searched the ditch, then shut off. Nothing moved under the bleachers. Total calm there . . . while a storm brewed in my head. Should I call the police station? There was no phone in my palace. Should I go there in person? To say what?—"They're here, they're here!" like they do in a puppet show? Who was "they," anyway? Apparently there was a hunter and some rabbits in this story. And you know what? In this kind of scenario, I always side with the rabbits.

Fifteen minutes went by before the truck started up and took off.

That was just what my rabbits were waiting for. Slowly they began to show the tips of their ears. I counted one, two, three . . . six. They were no longer running, but walked one behind the other along the sideline. They were holding something close to their chests, but I couldn't tell what. Finally

I saw them clearly enough to realize that they were carrying their clothes! They were half naked! And they were boys, maybe twelve or thirteen years old, as skinny as alley cats. From fifty feet away, I could count their ribs. They headed in my direction and stopped right beneath my window. For a moment, we stayed face to face: they shivered and looked bewildered, and I remained frozen behind the curtain. I was about to open the window when something struck me like a thunderbolt. The last boy in line, the tallest it seemed, was carrying a tiny child in his arms! He had wrapped him in a sweater, and poking from it, I could just make out a round head. Suddenly the child stuck out an arm and pointed forward. Immediately, they all took off in that direction. I've known a good many children in my life but none with such authority. It was a first.

I rushed into the kitchen to keep them in sight and found my all-star team behind the neighbor's house. At the bottom of a side door was a cat flap. The little one got dropped there and attempted to slip through. He managed to squeeze in up to his hips, but no amount of fidgeting helped him go farther. One of the boys tried to push the rest of him through and got a swift kick in the face. The others looked on without laughing. Finally, the little one wriggled out, turned himself around and disappeared inside the cat flap feetfirst. A few seconds later, the door opened and they all hurried in.

They were hardly inside when the rain started pouring again. My eyes stayed glued to the door. My small-time thief was now light-years away from my thoughts.

# eight

ACCOUNT OF AGATHE MERLE,

SEVENTY-FOUR YEARS OLD

Squirrels, according to Maurice! Squirrels indeed! The poor guy sure isn't improving with age. Have you ever heard of squirrels opening a jar of jam? Maybe a bag of cookies, since they can nibble the wrapping, but my jar of rhubarb jam? No way. I could ask the neighbor if any disturbance occurred over at his house, but I don't dare disturb him. He's a writer. I know that through François, the great-great-nephew of poor Germaine. He's here for two or three weeks, this man. He needs to work in quiet surroundings and is not to be bothered. So I won't. But I could tell him a lot of stories. We're definitely not short on stories around here.

As for the jar of jam, I don't share my suspicions with anyone. They would laugh in my face. But I remain adamant: what creature with nimble fingers could have squeezed through the cat flap and opened the jam? You can turn the question round and round but if you have two cents' worth of common sense, you'll come to the same conclusion I did: it was a monkey. A monkey, I tell you. A monkey that escaped from a circus. Very simple.

In the meantime, I'll ask Maurice to nail the cat flap shut. The cat will just have to use its litter box from now on.

# nine

I wouldn't mind walking if I had my own shoes. But I lost one of them in the ditch after we got out of the truck, and the others didn't let me look for it. So I found a pair of ladies' shoes in the garage where we slept, and now I wear them to walk with. Max keeps laughing at me 'cause of the heels. Very funny!

It was nice in the garage. We dried our clothes over the boiler and slept in overalls that we found there. There weren't enough for each of us, so the older twins took turns wearing a pair. Max and I were allowed to keep ours all night long. Before leaving, we ate three packs of cookies and some sort of jam I'd never had before. We took care to put everything back in place, overalls and all. We also pinched a canvas bag, the kind you take for grocery shopping. Fabien and Rémy traded off carrying it 'cause of Yann. He must weigh at least twenty-five pounds. They said we would be easily noticed with him, that six kids and a little guy like Yann would attract attention. So they put him in the bag. Only, now we have to carry him.

We left in three groups of two. Fabien and Rémy walked ahead. They went fast and it wasn't easy to keep up. They stopped only when they didn't know which way to go. When that happened, they put the bag down and Yann stuck his little head out. He turned it around in all directions like a periscope; he looked up as if he were sniffing the air; then he pointed his finger and we were on our way again. Pierre and Paul, the middle twins, followed a hundred yards behind with their caps hugging their heads, the earflaps bobbing on the sides. Now and then, they glanced back to see if we were coming. Of course we were coming. We didn't have a choice. We're the youngest ones, so we follow. But we're really brave, Rémy said so. We only cried a little when we left the house in the middle of the night. At last, the rain stopped today, which is good.

It was midmorning when the older twins waited for us and together we went to a sort of shed by the roadside. I think it was a bus shelter.

"Where are we going, Rémy?" I asked.

It was a question I'd been wanting to ask for a while.

"We're going west. Toward the ocean," he said.

"The Atlantic Ocean," Fabien added.

He took a bag of cookies from his pocket. That was a nice surprise 'cause I thought we had eaten them all. As we nibbled in silence, Fabien's words swirled in the shelter:

"*Atlantic Ocean . . . Atlantic Ocean . . .*"

The people passing by in their cars gave us dirty looks, but they weren't going as far as we were. Yann stayed hidden; he ate in his bag. He just brushed the crumbs off so that they wouldn't scratch him.

The Atlantic Ocean. I don't know how long it takes to get there, and I don't know what we'll do once we get there. . . . But for at least one hour, Max and I felt less tired. Afterward, we walked cheerfully. Max even wore my ladies' shoes for a mile or two. But I saw that they were hurting him so I switched back.

# ten

ACCOUNT OF MAX DOUTRELEAU,
ELEVEN YEARS OLD, YANN'S BROTHER

I tried to give Victor a break by wearing his shoes, but after a mile my toes felt like jelly. I don't know how he managed to walk in them. Guess it's better than going barefoot.

Around noon, a car passed us with a woman and two kids at the back. They were about our age, probably being picked up from school. They turned around and made faces at Victor and me. We ignored them. They did the same thing when they passed the middle twins, but Paul gave them the Italian elbow gesture and Pierre gave them the finger, which is worse. Someday Pierre and Paul will meet some real tough guys and get a good whipping. That's what the older twins always tell them. But Pierre and Paul don't listen. You'd think they beat up others to make up for all the beatings they've taken from the father. That it's their revenge. It's funny 'cause they have square heads. I wonder whether their heads became square 'cause they're violent or whether they became violent 'cause of their square heads. In any case, their heads suit them. At school, they fear no one. The first day Victor and I started sixth grade, an older boy made fun of us. He was snatching our caps and calling us by each other's names like it was a big joke.

"To my right Doutreleau, to my left Loutredeau, huh, no, to my left . . ."

Everyone who was looking on was laughing. Victor and I were also smiling 'cause we didn't want to cry on our first day.

Then Pierre and Paul came by. They didn't waste any time trying to find out the why and how, or the age of the boy. They didn't say a word. They went right into action. Swinging their book bags at arm's length, they hit the bully. The boy fell down but Pierre and Paul didn't stop. They pounded him good. His mouth was bleeding and one of the supervisors stopped the beating. The school punished them and the father gave them a good bashing on top of it. But that very evening, when we went to bed, Pierre came over to us.

"If anyone bothers you again, you tell us," he said.

We were surprised 'cause Pierre and Paul rarely talk to us. They keep to themselves, they do.

Anyway, no one bothered us again.

I thought about that while I looked at them walking ahead of us, the flaps of their caps bobbing on the sides. I wondered if they would really be able to beat up everyone who wanted to hurt us. Weren't they still too young for that?

We finally arrived near a village. It was almost one by the steeple clock. We hid in a small forest next to the village. The older twins put the bag down and told us to wait for them. They were going to get some food and would be back right away.

# eleven

ACCOUNT OF MICHÈLE MOULIN,
FORTY-TWO YEARS OLD, BAKER

I was about to close the shop when they walked in. Two tall, pale boys with crumpled jackets. Twins. You can say what you want but when two people look identical, it's striking. It's like magic. You can even imagine that they might disappear in a puff of smoke, then reappear in miniature and in four replicas, or as one twelve-foot-tall person. You think they're probably able to accomplish wonders and that if they don't, it's just because they're modest.

Could even their mother tell these two apart? Probably. No doubt she knew the secret, the almost invisible difference between them: a slight swaying of the head in one, a certain mischievousness in the eye of the other. How can you figure it out? They say twins are even more alike on rainy days. That is another one of their mysteries.

They took only a small step inside the shop, then stopped. I didn't know which one to look at.

"Good day, ma'am," one of them said very quietly. "We would like some bread but we have no money."

I made him repeat himself because I was unsure of what I had heard. But the words were the same.

"Good day, ma'am, we would like some bread but we have no money."

Then I understood why they stayed near the door. They weren't paying customers, so they didn't want to come in any farther. That's what moved me, I believe, this shyness. As well as their clothes. They seemed like really poor kids.

I've owned this shop for seven years, and before that, I owned one in Angoulême. In all this time no one has ever asked me for a handout with such sincerity and innocence.

I didn't have to think long.

"No problem," I answered.

I handed them a loaf of bread. The boy on the left stepped forward and took it. Then without thinking, I did what anybody else would have done: I took a second loaf of bread and handed it to his brother.

They thanked me and left. I closed the door behind them and went upstairs to eat.

The following week, when the first article on the Doutreleaus appeared in the newspaper, I put two and two together. I think the ones I met were the older twins. I think that because of their gentleness. The middle twins were said to be violent, quite violent. The reporter wrote that it had taken several men to restrain them and that one of the police officer's fingers got twisted. But there's a big gap between what they write in the newspapers and the truth. . . . In any case, the twins I gave bread to didn't seem dangerous. They were merely sad-looking. Now, the smaller ones must have hidden somewhere near the village while they waited for their brothers to return with food. As for Yann, I'd rather not say anything. So many stupidities have already been uttered. It's as if people didn't hear enough fairy tales in their childhood and try to catch up years later. In my bakery, a lot of gossip goes around and I've heard it all.

"Yes, yes, Mrs. Moulin, the kid was a genius. He could beat a computer at chess. . . ."

"One hardly dares say so, Mrs. Moulin, but the child was retarded. His brothers were so ashamed of him, which is why they hid him in a bag. . . ."

"By the way, did you know that the kid could see in the dark same as a cat?"

"People say he never slept. . . ."

"People say he was always sleeping. . . ."

"He was six years old." "He was twelve." "He was three. . . ."

I won't even try to tell you the worst of the gossip. I let them talk. The only truth is that "this kid," as they say, was just a kid. A little kid. A kid who asked only to be kept warm and longed to hear some loving words now and again. Like any other kid. I don't know much about this affair, but I've got the feeling that he never experienced any of that. So people should leave him alone and hold their idle tongues.

Especially now that he's no longer here.

My only consolation is that the little one probably ate a bit of my bread, and that I offered it with all my heart.

# twelve

ACCOUNT OF PIERRE DOUTRELEAU,
THIRTEEN YEARS OLD, YANN'S BROTHER

The older ones came back some ten minutes later with two loaves of bread.

"Someone gave these to us," they said.

"Is that all?" I asked.

That was all. Paul looked at me and we understood each other. Next time me and him would take charge of bringing back real food. But we didn't say anything 'cause this wasn't the time to quarrel. We shared equally and started to eat standing up. Then we all sat down in a circle on the ground. It was wet, but we didn't mind 'cause our legs were heavy from walking all morning. Besides, we had all afternoon to dry off. In the middle of the circle, Yann stayed in the bag. He nibbled a piece of bread and went to sleep. We all looked at him silently. It was funny 'cause it looked like the crèche with baby Jesus. Except that there was no menagerie around Yann, no donkey, or ox, or any other beast, only us eating our bread.

# thirteen

ACCOUNT OF PAUL DOUTRELEAU,
THIRTEEN YEARS OLD, YANN'S BROTHER

We waited a good quarter of an hour in the forest, hopping from one foot to the other, before Rémy and Fabien finally came back with something to eat. But their "something to eat" was two measly loaves of bread! Pierre and I looked at each other. It was understood that next time me and him would take charge of the refueling efforts, which would be to everybody's advantage. We sat down on the ground to eat. It didn't matter that we drenched our butts;

we'd had it with standing up. Yann ate nothing. Maybe a morsel, but not even half of his share. We put him in the middle in his bag and he went to sleep. I threw my jacket over him 'cause when you sleep it's nice to be warm. We looked at him for a good while.

I said nothing but I thought it looked like the crèche with baby Jesus inside.

# fourteen

ACCOUNT OF DOMINIQUE ETCHEVERRY,
TWENTY-EIGHT YEARS OLD, POLICE OFFICER

It was strange. It had been quiet all morning; then around one o'clock in the afternoon, the parade began. First a nice old lady entered, claiming that someone had poisoned her dog. She was barely out the door when a guy in his twenties strolled in, carrying a motorcycle helmet under his arm.

"Good morning, sir. I want to file a complaint," he said.

An old nut had supposedly tried to push him off

the road with his car. He had hardly finished explaining the details of the encounter when the door swung open and in came what looked like a couple of peasants from the Middle Ages.

"Can you wait a bit?" I asked them.

The man lifted his large hand as a sign that yes, they could wait, there was no rush. The woman seemed to agree. In fact, it turned out to be urgent but I couldn't have guessed.

"Sit down!" I told them, motioning to the couch by the door.

No reaction. They were the type of people who sit only on wooden chairs or on a bench. As soon as the seating is soft, or low, they think they'll dirty the thing or that they won't be able to get up. It isn't for them. So they remained standing.

I went next door with the motorcyclist, and

when I was through with him, I came back to the reception area. The couple had not budged. I bet they hadn't even exchanged a single word.

"Ma'am, sir?" I greeted them.

The man elbowed the woman forward.

She came near me. "It's the kids," she said. "They scrammed."

"Excuse me?"

"The kids . . . they scrammed."

She heaved two big sobs. Like hiccups. It didn't last long. She must have hated herself for showing her feelings and was instantly cold as stone again. The situation must have taken a toll on her and explaining things had clearly shaken her.

The man looked at us fiercely as if to say, "I agreed to follow the mother here, but she's the one who does the talking. Don't ask me nothin'."

The "kids," as she said, had left in the night. In any case, come this morning they were gone. And why would they go? She didn't know. Was it the first time they had run away? Yes, the first time. Couldn't they simply be at school? No, they weren't at school. And it was only now that they reported it? Yes, 'cause they searched for them brats before coming. . . .

I gather it's true that they must have searched. Both of them looked distraught; their hair was tousled, their clothes dripping wet. They would have had a hard time trying to convince anyone that they were coming from a bridge party at the mayor's house.

I wrote up a report, called my partner over, and we jumped in our car. The Doutreleaus, that's their name, drove in front of us in their jalopy, which, among other things, was missing the rear bumper and the side mirror.

In the courtyard of their farm was a red car, along with two people who watched us approach.

# fifteen

ACCOUNT OF PASCAL JOSSE,
THIRTY-FOUR YEARS OLD, MECHANIC,
NATHALIE JOSSE'S HUSBAND

It was the first time Nathalie did that to me. In the middle of the night, she had an awful nightmare.

"Get me out of here!" she shouted. "Get me out of here!" She dug her nails into my arm.

I was only too glad to get her out of wherever she was, but she had to cooperate a little. The most urgent was to wake her completely. I turned on the light, took her face in my hands and stroked it gently.

"Wake up, Nathalie . . . it's me!"

Nothing doing. Apparently her invisible ene-mies seemed bent on keeping her in their grip. I would have gladly disemboweled, crushed and beheaded them, but it wasn't easy to know who they were. She finally opened her eyes. My face was the first thing she saw and she was so happy, apparently, that she threw herself upon me and held me tight. Like a drowning person would do with a buoy. It's at times like this that you have the pleasant feeling of being useful. The customers at the garage where I work don't show their appreciation in any similar fashion, that's for sure.

"You had a nightmare," I told her. "Everything is fine now. Calm down."

I kept her pressed against me to calm her further. I told her sweet things, but that is not the point. . . .

Ten minutes later, we were seated in the kitchen, drinking cups of hot milk, and she was telling me about her nightmare, one that involved an intelligent little boy and his six twin brothers. It reminded me of a particular story.

"Say, isn't that the tale of Tom Thumb you're telling me?"

She seemed startled and yet it was evident, don't you think? I'm not a literary genius but I know my classics. I even remembered that in Perrault's tale, the mother loved one of the older twins better than the other because his hair was more reddish. She was a redhead herself. I retained this fact because my own hair is red. Actually, not so much red as flamelike. So we had all the characters in the story: the six brothers, all twins, and the last one, the little shrimp the size of a thumb, who of course was to become the center of the tale. Only the nasty character, the ogre, was missing from the cast. But apparently my wife had just met him, which explained her agitated state.

"The worst is that the little kid had his eyes fixed on me," she was saying. "He was enduring horrible things and all he did was look at me as if to say, 'See what you've done? Nice job, right?' "

I'll spare you the details of the horrible treatment inflicted on the child in Nathalie's nightmare. Too gruesome to talk about.

To reassure her, I promised to accompany her to the farm the next day. That's why we were both in the Doutreleaus' courtyard around one-thirty in the afternoon.

"You can stay in the car, but I'd like you to be there," Nathalie said. "That woman scares me."

The yard was exactly as Nathalie had described it. The Doutreleaus clearly didn't have a subscription to *House & Garden*.

The dog stood on the threshold. His head was cocked at an angle and he squinted a lot; Nathalie had forgotten to tell me that. Other than the dog, there was no one around, tall or small. It was a Tuesday; the children were probably at school. But where were the parents? I blew my horn once, then twice. The dog watched us silently. His bent head didn't make him out to be gleaming with intelligence, if you see what I mean.

I got out of the car and went toward the shed to see if a car was inside. Only a beat-up-looking tractor. I was about to turn around when I heard the mewing. The kittens had to be very small. Where were they hiding? I'm curious by nature. Nathalie always complains about it. I always have to see and to know. I can't resist. So I listened carefully, trying to locate the little mewing fellows, and after a minute I was telling myself, "You're hot. You're very hot. You're burning." I found them at the back of a closet, or what was left of it. Seven kittens still blind, crawling on top of each other, all crying for food. The mother was probably nearby. I crouched and observed the litter forlornly. I'm a country boy and I know what fate awaited them: seven kittens born on a farm like this have a dim chance of staying alive. In the best scenario, it's chloroform, a bag . . . and the river. In the worst case, it's two blows to the head with a shovel, and a third one if they still move. Not for sensitive souls. I was tempted to take one of them, to spare it that fate, but what would we have done with it? We can't keep a cat in the apartment with the baby. At that moment, their mother arrived and lay down on top of them.

*Take advantage of this!* I thought. *You'll never know more of life than the warmth of your mother's belly, but better that than nothing.*

Nathalie had come to the door of the shed. "What are you doing? If someone sees you—"

Right then, two cars entered the yard. In the first were the Doutreleau parents. The other was a police car.

The eyes of the Doutreleau father were on me in a flash. "What the hell are you doing here?" he seemed to be asking.

I realized then that eyes could actually say this: "What the hell are you doing here?"

"I'm sorry," I mumbled as he got out of his car and walked over. "We were waiting for you and I heard mewing in the shed, so I went in to see."

"Yeah, that's right, them cats," he said absent-mindedly. "I wanted to kill 'em this mornin', but with everythin' that's goin' on . . ."

"Goin' on?" we wondered. One of the officers asked us who we were. When he heard that Nathalie was a social worker, he took her aside and explained that the seven children had disappeared, that all of them had left during the night. Then the officers went inside the house with the Doutreleaus. Nathalie and I had no more reason to be there, so we left. Nathalie cried all the way back home.

I spent the afternoon in the garage shop. I couldn't concentrate and hope I didn't install too many brake pads in reverse. I didn't see carburetors or batteries or spark plugs; I saw seven kittens, seven little Doutreleaus and seven Tom Thumbs. All this was swirling in my head. I remembered a picture from my childhood very clearly—a picture of Tom Thumb shown hiding under a stool during the terrible night. The father was saying, "I've decided to lose them in the wood tomorrow." The mother was holding her face in her hands. A meager fire was burning in the fireplace.

I was driving home when it hit me. Like a thunderbolt.

And what if . . . what if little Yann . . . or one of his brothers, but no, it could only be him, I could feel it; what if little Yann had heard his father say in the night:

"I'll kill 'em all tomorrow! All seven of 'em!"

And what if he had thought that his father wanted . . .

You were mistaken, little Yann! You, the know-it-all, you who understood everything, for once you made a mistake!

Kill all seven of *them*! Yes. But the seven *cats*, Yann! The *cats*! Not you and your brothers! The *cats*!

Where are you now so we can tell you? Where have you dragged your brothers to?

# PART TWO

Alas, poor children, where have you come to?
Don't you know that this is the Ogre's house—
the one who eats little children?
—"Tom Thumb," Charles Perrault

# one

ACCOUNT OF FABIEN DOUTRELEAU,
FOURTEEN YEARS OLD, YANN'S BROTHER

In the morning, several cars slowed down when passing us, and we were afraid we'd be caught. Even in separate groups, people noticed us. Even with Yann in the bag. Once we'd eaten our bread in the forest, Rémy, me and the middle twins had a talk. We couldn't risk following the road any longer or we wouldn't get far. We'd get caught. And if they caught us, they'd take us back home. Whatever we'd say to the police to explain why we left, they'd never believe us. And once the police left, the father would give us a good beating, then do what Yann said . . . kill the seven of us.

We never talk about it. Not when we walk and not when we stop for a break. We're not allowed. It's like a dirty word, impossible to say. Even the little ones understand and follow without questioning. Or maybe they question where we're going, but not why.

"We're going west, to the ocean," Rémy told them in the bus shelter this morning.

"The Atlantic Ocean," I added.

There was silence and we all saw the ocean, heard the waves crash on the sand, and felt the wind on our skin. I even got goose bumps.

Another time, Victor asked when we would get there, and that question was not easy to answer.

If we abandoned the road and traveled only on the back lanes, we wouldn't be arriving at the ocean anytime soon. The distance is twice as long. The only advantage was that Yann could come out of the bag, which would give Rémy and me a break, especially Rémy, who seems dead tired. We would only have to hide Yann in case of danger or when he'd be too exhausted to walk. As for which direction to go in, it wouldn't change anything considering that with Yann it's easy: he has a compass in his head, or antennas, or I don't know what. In any case, he never hesitates for long, just lifts his little head toward the sky and turns it around in all directions before pointing with his finger. And we follow.

I was intrigued by this.

"How do you do it?" I asked him when we reached a crossroads.

*The light,* he told me. *The light in the sky is clearer to the west.*

I, for one, see no difference.

# two

ACCOUNT OF RÉMY DOUTRELEAU,
FOURTEEN YEARS OLD, YANN'S BROTHER

We left the road. It's better 'cause we can all walk together and Fabien and me don't have to carry the bag. Our arms and shoulders were beginning to ache. Each of us held one handle of the bag, as if coming back from shopping. But even though we changed sides every hundred yards, it still hurt our fingers a lot. Now we're getting a break, especially Fabien, who isn't as strong as me.

We followed the dirt paths, the undergrowth,

the riverbanks. Sometimes it was wide enough for us to walk together at a brisk clip; sometimes it was narrower and we walked single file. When we lost our way in the tall grasses, we put Yann on our shoulders and got out of there drenched with dew. Whenever we got discouraged we had the feeling we'd never reach any place, that even if we wore our legs out walking, it would be for nothing. But none of us wanted to be the first to complain, so we stayed silent and kept going.

Sometimes we were rewarded. Late in the afternoon, for instance, we followed a towpath along a canal going west. It was pleasant. The ground was dry, we weren't too cold or too hot, or anything. Without even thinking about it, we began to walk faster, as if the canal were leading straight to the ocean and we'd reach it before dark if we hustled along. We knew this wasn't true, but it was comforting to think that way.

At one point we all relieved ourselves behind a thicket, used dead leaves for wiping and washed our hands in the canal. The water wasn't warm. Soon after, darkness descended and the cold fell upon us. We walked a little farther but the path narrowed quickly and ended in a patch of nettles. We had to retrace our steps for half a mile, where we sat on a bridge and leaned our backs against a small stone wall.

The middle twins had their grim-eyed bad-day faces on, and since they were both sucking the straps of their caps, it was obvious that they were hungry.

The little twins seemed tired too.

"Where are we going to sleep?" Victor asked as he took off his ladies' shoes.

We saw that both his feet had ugly red stripes

across the top. He was really brave not to complain. Especially since his ankles were covered with white blisters from the nettle burns. No one answered him, so he began to cry silently. I pretended not to see and the others did the same. We had nothing to nurse his feet with, anyway. If we had tried to comfort him, his tears would only have doubled. It was better to pretend not to see.

We were in this great predicament when Yann lifted his finger.

*Do you hear?*

Nope. We did not hear. Except for Victor's sniffling and the *flop* of a frog jumping into the canal, we heard nothing. But Yann kept his finger in the air, so we pricked our ears and finally heard it too. It was a muffled rumble, from far away. Then we saw a streak of light on the horizon, a long red line in the dark of the countryside.

A train was traveling full speed in the night. And it was headed west.

# three

**ACCOUNT OF COLETTE FAURE,**
**SEVENTY-EIGHT YEARS OLD, RETIRED**

People don't believe me when I tell them. They should spend time in my home. For one, I'd have company. And two, they'd see that I'm not lying. I challenge you to watch the railroad tracks for more than half a day and not see someone walking along. That surprises you! Yet it's the truth, nothing but the truth.

I've been looking at that railroad track for fifteen years. I've got a chair by the window. To the right is the TV set, to the left the track. I sit between the two, looking sometimes right, sometimes left, sometimes at the TV, sometimes at the track. When I tire of it all, I feed the cat and watch him eat his food.

With the number of roads, highways and such, I wonder why people need to walk here. But I've my own idea by now. They walk here because it's a straight line and because at the end is always a station. These are sure things, and they provide comfort. Usually, it's a lonely soul, walking with head low, feeling down and out. At least, I suppose so. Why else would anyone walk alone along the track, unless they were depressed?

Sometimes I want to open my window and shout out to them: "Things won't improve! Why don't you lie down on the rail; the next train comes in five minutes! At last, you'll have peace!" It makes me laugh. I'm not nasty, just a bit of a tease. You entertain yourself the way you can. It comes with age. My mind wasn't so twisted before. . . .

I don't think such thoughts when the person is young. And not if it's dark. The young ones passed by at eleven at night. The news came on the TV, so I knew the time. Four fellows walked single file, with a funny-looking little boy in front. The moon was full and I could see them as clearly as I can see you. Imagine a little boy with a jacket straight out of the 1950s, buttoned down the middle. Waddling like a penguin on a field of ice, he took three steps for every single step of his companions. Fifty yards behind came a sixth boy, carrying another one on his back.

I waited to see if any others showed up but they

were the last ones. The parade had ended. As they passed by my house, the boy who was being carried looked in my direction for a good while. I motioned to him with my chin: "You want my picture or what?"

Périgueux is more than twenty miles away. *Kids*, I said to myself, *if you want to be there before daybreak, you'd better pick up the pace.*

When they spoke about these boys in the following week's newspapers, I instantly called the police. They didn't listen to me. For one, the kids had been found. And two, no one ever listens to me.

# four

## ACCOUNT OF MAX DOUTRELEAU,
### ELEVEN YEARS OLD, YANN'S BROTHER

"We're there," Fabien said. "Only one more mile. The town is called Périgueux. We'll walk to the station and take the train."

The sun was just rising. On each side of the track, gray houses gradually appeared out of the mist. Inside, people were probably sleeping snugly. Had Fabien said ten more miles, or one hundred twenty, or four million? It made no difference to Victor and me. We looked down at our legs to see if they hadn't been worn out up to the knee. But they were intact and we continued to plow ahead like robots. I wondered if our legs would obey and stop when we asked them to.

There was a large square in front of the railroad station. We hid close to garbage cans. The oldest and the middle twins talked things over among them—and with Yann, of course. Meanwhile Victor and me huddled close together 'cause we were cold now that we had stopped walking. I understood why the big ones seemed cautious: none of us had ever boarded a train and they didn't know how to go about getting tickets. It's probably easy, but when you don't know . . .

Finally, Pierre took the shopping bag and tore it open about four inches on one side, and Yann climbed in. Pierre secured the bag under his arm and both of them entered the station. A clock displayed the time: seven-thirty. When they came back, it was exactly eight o'clock. Pierre handed us tickets to Bordeaux. There were only three, but as Pierre said, "When you are twins, it's enough for six."

# five

ACCOUNT OF VICTOR DOUTRELEAU,
ELEVEN YEARS OLD, YANN'S BROTHER

It didn't smell too good next to the garbage cans, but at least we were no longer walking. I wedged myself against Max, back to back, and we tried to warm ourselves while we waited for the big ones to decide on a plan. I closed my eyes: cars were stopping, others were taking off, I could hear the banging of doors. It was like in a dream. Maybe that's how you feel after a sleepless night. The day before, I cried a little near the stone bridge. I would've liked to be more courageous, but I couldn't help it. Not 'cause my feet were hurting or 'cause of the nettles, but 'cause I was certain I'd be the first who wouldn't be able to go any farther. And since my brothers would never abandon me, everyone would have to stop. We'd never reach the ocean that way. And it would be my fault.

Luckily, that's when we saw the train go by. It gave us hope and we got on our way again. Paul carried me on his back for about a mile. At some point, we passed in front of a lighted house. A fat woman opened the curtain and glared at me.

"You want my picture?" I mumbled.

"What?" Paul asked.

"Nothing," I said, 'cause he hadn't seen the woman and it was too long to explain. Anyway, it didn't matter.

Farther up, Paul fell and hurt his knee. That's the way he is, Paul: he says he's not tired, then he plods on until he falls. I felt ashamed, so I started to walk again.

When we reached Périgueux, it was daylight and my feet didn't hurt anymore. The red stripes on my feet had turned black and a little blue too. I think I went to sleep next to the garbage cans. I must have been really tired, considering the stench and the cold.

I only remember that Pierre tore the bag with his hands and put Yann inside and off they went into the station.

# six

ACCOUNT OF VALÉRIE MASSAMBA,
TWENTY-FIVE YEARS OLD, STUDENT

That's the way I am. I'm so afraid of missing the train that I always come to the station at least forty-five minutes ahead of time. And I hang out. Usually I find a seat on a bench and stick my nose in a magazine. It sends the message that I don't want to be bothered.

That's why when the boy sat right in front of me, I didn't notice him at first.

It's the smell that caught my attention. I don't know when this kid had last changed socks, but you didn't need a hunting dog to follow his scent. *Mamma mia!* If he had been an adult I would have changed seats right away. But he was about twelve or thirteen, not more, and it was sad to see how he was dressed: a brown parka that no longer closed, threads of wool hanging from the sleeves of a sweater. The only acceptable item was a cap with earflaps that made him look like an airplane pilot of the past. On his knees, he had one of those canvas bags used for grocery shopping. Strange piece of luggage to travel with.

I had the feeling that this kid did not like to be tickled; you could guess that from his chiseled face, his square chin. Nevertheless there was something fragile in his eyes, something restless. I'm an immigrant and I know that look well. I see it in my own mirror. So, in spite of the smell, I stayed in my seat.

At that point, I was far from guessing how inter-
esting things would become.

I'll try to be clear because it would be easy to lose
the thread. Really!

To begin with, something started to move in the
kid's bag. Was it a cat? A dog? A rabbit? A chicken? I
had no idea. The only thing I was sure of was
that *it* was alive! The kid bent forward and whispered
to the moving thing. He must love his pet a lot,
whether cat, turtle or canary, to talk to it like that!
Then he sat up, surveyed the travelers, and once again
leaned into the bag. This occurred ten times more.

Twenty minutes later, I hadn't moved. I continued to read my magazine. At least, I pretended to.

Suddenly the kid got up and walked toward a
bench where a father and his two youngsters, who
had just bought their tickets, were seated. The three

of them were fooling around, happy to be taking the train together, maybe for the first time. My scented kid walked up behind them, put down his bag next to theirs and positioned himself a few yards away, near the newspaper stand. From there, he made believe he was looking around, but he wanted to see the two bags so badly that he squinted. Someone else was also squinting—me, Valérie. What in the world was going on?

I was about to find out, and it was a sight to behold.

The canvas bag had a split along one side. Suddenly, out from the split emerged what looked like a small hose. The small hose turned out to be the sleeve of a jacket, and at the extremity of the jacket sleeve was a hand! Makes perfect sense, right?

The hand was very tiny and plump. It fumbled a bit, had a hard time finding the father's leather bag. From his spot near the newspaper stand, the boy made faces. If he could, he would have screamed, "To the left! To the left again! There you are!" Only he couldn't do that. All he could do was watch and suffer.

Finally the little hand reached its target.

*Zip!* It pulled on the bag's zipper!

It searched inside the bag and pulled out three train tickets.

*Zip* again! And the little hand disappeared where it had come from. That's it.

The boy didn't waste a second. He passed behind the bench again, grabbed the two handles of the shopping bag, walked straight toward the exit and vanished. Just in time. The father looked at the clock and gathered his youngsters. The three of them headed toward platform two, where the train for Bordeaux was departing from.

I know it's not right. I know I should have informed, reported, warned. I should have . . . but I didn't. Something in the boy's eyes reminded me too much of a trapped animal.

Fifteen minutes later, having barely recovered from the excitement, I settled in the express train, in the middle of a car, where the seats face each other. What I had witnessed—a kid using a smaller child to steal train tickets—was surprising; still, it made sense. What followed, though, plunged me into a sea of bewilderment. The boy appeared again, but he was no longer alone. Another boy, pale and as badly dressed, accompanied him, along with a younger kid of around ten, who I swear was wearing women's shoes! The boy no longer carried the shopping bag and he had changed his clothes: new shoes, new pants, new parka! Only the smell remained the same.

I love crosswords, puzzles, any game that forces me to think. The more difficult it is, the more determined I am. I guess that makes me someone who needs to understand things. For once, I had found a challenging mystery!

The three boys sat around me. The youngest one right next to me, looking as awed as if he were on board a space shuttle. The train had gone hardly half a mile when his head dropped back, his mouth opened as wide as a plate and he fell fast asleep. His women's shoes slipped off his feet. The older one, facing him, looked stupefied but did his best to hide it.

The middle boy, the one facing me, should have recognized me, but he didn't pay me any attention.

We were nearly midway to Bordeaux when the conductor appeared.

"Your tickets, please." He held out his hand toward the big pale boy. "Did you change seats?" he asked, puzzled.

The boy blushed. "Yes, was that wrong?" he mumbled.

"No . . . no, of course, you can."

The controller walked away. The two boys let out sighs of relief and exchanged a meaningful gaze. "It worked!" they seemed to be saying. "Let's stay put! Let's not attract attention!"

The guessing game became even more fascinating: why had the boy with the cap changed clothes? Why hadn't he shown his tickets? I knew he had them. And why had the older boy claimed to have already presented them? Where? When?

I was about to give up when a clue appeared: a boy advanced down the aisle, holding a sandwich in each hand. He looked feature for feature, hair for hair, like the one seated in front of me. He didn't linger. He quickly distributed the two snacks and off he went.

Twins! Everything was clear now! If the tall pale boy had a twin brother, the middle kid probably had one too! So it wasn't the little thief who was seated in front of me, but his brother. That was why he didn't have the same clothes, and why he hadn't recognized me. I turned to the younger boy, who was still asleep next to me. Could it be that he too . . . ? Curiosity got the better of me. I was eager to take a look in the adjoining car. . . .

There was nothing there and nothing in the next car either. I continued along until I reached the rear of the train. Here they were, the three of them!

Yes, I rightly say the three of them, for the youngest one also had an identical twin! He was sleeping on the seat, all curled up. One of the older boys had thrown a jacket over him. But this one didn't have women's shoes on.

One of the seats was unoccupied, and I sat down. My little thief with the cap recognized me. I smiled at him: "Hey, we know each other," I was saying. He smiled back, shyly. I had now assembled nearly all the pieces of the puzzle. Only one was missing: where was that little hand? To whom did the little hand belong? Where was the shopping bag?

The train shook us as it sped on. The answer arrived when I least expected it. My little thief betrayed himself when he took two peeks upward. It was one too many. What was there to see up there, tell me? In turn, I looked up.

The canvas bag was above our heads, among other pieces of luggage. The furtive little hand slipped through the opening. It searched, groped, danced, rummaged, stole and disappeared. But this time train tickets weren't what it was nimbly pinching. It was after a chocolate bar, a pack of cookies, a slice of bread and cheese.

This time my little thief noticed that I saw it all. He blushed, lowered his eyes, looked at me again and accepted my attention. We had a silent conversation:

Him: "You've seen everything, right?"

Me: "Yes, I've seen."

Him: "It's funny, isn't it?"

Me: "Yes, it's funny."

Him: "Please, don't say anything."

Me: "I will say nothing."

The little hand popped out again and tried to get

hold of an apple. The apple was too big; it slipped and was about to fall on one of the passengers' heads.

*Your other hand!* we shouted together silently. *Your other hand!*

The other hand appeared. The apple was grabbed; it didn't fall and disappeared into the canvas bag with the rest of the loot.

An hour ago, we hadn't known one another, and now we were allies.

I will say nothing because he and I are on the same side. Because he's not doing this for fun. Because he has a beautiful smile in spite of his square face. Maybe also because he placed a jacket over his sleeping younger brother.

# seven

ACCOUNT OF PIERRE DOUTRELEAU,
THIRTEEN YEARS OLD, YANN'S BROTHER

I got scared. If the others hadn't been waiting out-side in the cold, I would have chickened out. But I had promised, so I sat down on a bench, with Yann on my knees, and observed my surroundings. I know nothing about railroad stations and trains. But I pick things up fast: people buy their tickets at a booth, then wait and eventually put their tickets through a gadget that makes a noise. It probably punches a hole in the ticket. Then they board the train. That's it. There was a black girl seated in front of me, reading a magazine. She didn't pay attention to us, didn't even look up once. We needed three tickets, no more. Yann lifted them from the bag of a man I singled out. He did a great job. Nobody saw us.

We separated to board the train. One twin in each group. I stayed with Fabien and Max. We kept hold of the tickets. I also took Yann 'cause me and him were beginning to make a good team. In the car, I put him in the overhead luggage rack and he did quite a number for us. He found enough food for all of us to eat. Sometimes I moved him around. I only got scared when the black girl came in and sat near us. She kept looking at us, and eventually what was bound to happen happened: she saw the bag and saw

Yann's hand sticking out of it. She saw everything. But she said nothing. She even laughed along with us. I had never seen a black person in real life before. Well, if you ask me now, I'd say they're no worse than any others.

# eight

ACCOUNT FROM PAUL DOUTRELEAU,
THIRTEEN YEARS OLD, YANN'S BROTHER

Once on the train, Victor fell asleep right away. A black girl sat down opposite me. At the beginning she kept looking over. What did she want? I didn't know her! When the conductor came by, Rémy whispered to himself the sentence we had rehearsed.

"We already showed them to you. We changed seats," he said softly.

Of course, we didn't know whether Rémy had already shown the tickets to the conductor. It was a game of heads or tails! Well, it worked. Fabien didn't even have to say anything. The conductor was the one who spoke.

"Did you change seats?" he asked.

It took us a while to recover—until the moment Fabien entered our car. He brought us sandwiches too. Crusty bread with a good coat of butter, delicious ham, and even pickles cut lengthwise. What a sandwich! I never had anything so good in my life. And I knew that Yann was the one who had lifted them, which made them taste even better. I ate mine so fast that I bit the inside of my cheek. I kept a third of the sandwich for Victor when he woke up. Rémy did the same.

# nine

ACCOUNT OF GÉRARD FARMANGEON,
FORTY-EIGHT YEARS OLD, SHOPKEEPER

In the morning I drink coffee. Nothing else goes down my throat. So when I have to spend the day in Bordeaux as I did the other day, I bring along a snack that I eat on the train come nine o'clock. It's my treat. I prepare my ham sandwiches with care. I prepare them that same morning so the bread is crusty, and I spare neither butter nor pickles. I did just that this morning and put them in a plastic bag.

"Can you put them in my carry-on?" I told Josiane.

"Sure, I'll put them in your carry-on," she answered.

Right before leaving, I checked with her again.

"Did you put them in my bag?"

"Did I put what in your bag?"

"The ham sandwiches! Did you put them in my bag?"

"Yes! I put them in your carry-on!" she said, getting annoyed. "Now get going or you'll miss your train."

Well, do you know what? The sandwiches were not in my bag.

# ten

ACCOUNT OF FABIEN DOUTRELEAU,
FOURTEEN YEARS OLD, YANN'S BROTHER

At the Bordeaux station, we almost missed each other in the crowd. Luckily the others headed toward the exit just as we did. That's where we regrouped. Turns out Bordeaux isn't by the ocean. Not one bit. You think it is if you don't look at the map closely, but it's not. It's at least thirty miles from Bordeaux to the ocean, as the crow flies.

"Never mind! Let's take another train!" said Pierre.

Nothing stops Pierre. He had succeeded in getting us tickets and food, so now he thought he was our leader and that none of us would put up a fuss. We were all seated on the ground trying to think of what to do next, while he paced in front of us.

"What are you waiting for?" he seemed to be saying. "I'm going back there, that's all."

I was convinced that we would get caught if we tried to board another train. It was already a miracle that we had made it this far, so why tempt fate? I was thinking about all the ground we'd covered since we left. About the truck that had taken us through the night, about our day on the road, about our long walk along the railroad track. I didn't want all our efforts to go to waste.

I also knew that there was only one leader among us and it was Yann.

I leaned toward the bag. "What do we do now?" I asked him.

He hesitated a bit. *Are the little ones tired?*

"They're okay, they slept on the train."

*Did they eat?*

"Yes, they ate."

*Can you and Rémy still carry me?*

"Of course."

He smiled and sheepishly trotted his middle and forefinger along the bag. We would walk, at least to get out of Bordeaux.

The middle twins made a face. They usually scowl when everything is fine, but now their faces took the prize. We set out again.

It took us more than two hours to reach the county road that led to the ocean. I guess Yann's compass wasn't very accurate in town, so we zig-zagged for a while.

Without asking anyone's opinion, Paul stuck out his thumb and got lucky: a pickup truck stopped. It looked like the one that used to come to our farm to sell supplies and groceries. That truck came on Thursdays, I remember. You could find everything from brooms to toothpaste to flyswatters, not to mention the famous "surprises." These were hidden in paper cones that came in two sizes: big and small. I still don't know what was inside since the mother never bought any, big or small.

"It's junk!" she used to say.

The truck came to our yard every Thursday for years. Then one day it stopped coming. Guess I wouldn't have bothered either since the mother never bought anything. The grocer's only reward for making the detour: Corniaud never failed to pee on the wheels of his truck.

One day, even if I'm grown up, I'll go to a store where they carry paper cones and I'll buy one of those surprises. If someone asks, "Is it for your kids?" I won't be ashamed to answer, "No, it's for me!" See, I don't want children. I'd rather enjoy a little bit of quiet later on. I'd keep Yann if I had to, though. We'll see.

"Where are you going?" the driver asked.

Paul answered that we were headed to the ocean.

"Well, then climb in the back!"

The man got out to open the door. I didn't know anyone could be so fat. He had to keep his legs wide apart so that his thighs didn't rub against each other too much.

# eleven

ACCOUNT OF EMILE DUCROCQ,
FIFTY YEARS OLD, GROCER

Yes, I'm the one who took the six Doutreleaus to the ocean. The seventh one too, I guess. But I never saw him, the little one. He was hidden in the famous bag. I crammed them all into the back and told them not to touch anything. They looked harmless as they sat among the groceries on the floor, and they didn't move. One of the two boys with caps sat with me in front, but he wasn't particularly talkative.

"So you're going to the ocean?"

"Yes."

"Where do you live? In Bordeaux?"

"Yes."

Since I'm not a chatterbox myself, we said nothing more for a good while. It was enough time to realize that the kid didn't smell like a rose. But what of it? I'm prone to having stinking feet, so we were on equal ground. In the glove compartment, I keep a map of the area. He took it and studied it carefully. Suddenly he pointed to a spot with his finger.

"That's where we're going!" he said.

He was pointing to the road along the ocean, his finger right on the house belonging to that madman. But I didn't know that the guy was mad! I heard about it later. There was no sign on the house indicating "Madman Lives Here." I wish they would stop bugging me to death now with this story! It was a

Wednesday. I thought the kids just wanted to see the beach, to take a stroll on the sand, not that they were runaways. I dropped them in front of the house, I can't deny it. They were nice kids, definitely not vandals. Since they hadn't touched any of the produce at the back, I even offered them something.

"Do you like bananas, kids?" I asked, giving one to each of them.

The cops blamed me for transporting passengers in my truck. I'm not licensed to do so. Well, I know I'm not allowed! I don't want to hear any more about it. In the grocery store, when customers mention the incident, I clam up.

"Will that be all?" I say quietly as I look them in the eye.

That shuts them up good.

# twelve

ACCOUNT OF THIERRY VIARD,
TWENTY-EIGHT YEARS OLD, UNEMPLOYED

My job is to keep an eye on Mr. Faivre's house. Two or three times a week I check that everything is "in order," to use his favorite expression. At the end of each month he gives me a hundred or a hundred and fifty dollars, depending on his mood. It pays for my cigarettes and since I pass in front of his ugly house anyway, I might as well get paid for it. Every evening I run on the beach, six, eight miles, it depends. I put my old sweats on, a hat on my head in winter, and I run. Since

I'm unemployed I try to run regularly; it cleanses my mind, relaxes me, otherwise I become angry.

Mr. Faivre isn't the type to get angry. I've never seen him mad. Not even irritated. His voice is so low that you don't catch half of what he says, which forces you to keep silent. It must please him to be listened to in silence. When he greets you, he extends a limp, unbelievably soft, fragile hand that doesn't squeeze yours. It's so unpleasant that I feel like shaking him, like crushing his fingers. He reminds me of a fish, except that even fish probably feel some emotion from time to time. Also, fish don't dabble in politics.

"I trust you implicitly, Thierry," he tells me, though it makes me shudder whenever he says that. I should be flattered but . . . It was at the beginning of fall when he handed me the keys to his house. His eyes, half closed, seemed to warn silently, "Don't you try to deceive me, you twerp."

There are hundreds of houses like his around here. The owners are rich people who spend two months out of the year by the seashore and the rest of the time live in fear of having their summer homes "visited." Faivre's house is sinister-looking, gray, with metallic electric shutters that make the place look as cheerful as a closed coffin. Guess it resembles its owner. He comes here in the summer with his wife and daughters. He's got a brood of daughters, more than five in any case. All of them blond and bursting with good health. Some of them are twins.

The road passes in front of the house. At the back, you've got the beach and the ocean. I've never been inside. I only walk around the property and make sure that everything is "in order"; then I continue running.

I noticed the kids around six o'clock in the evening. It was November, when the summer crowd is long gone, so six kids on the beach are noticeable. I thought they were Gypsies because of their clothes, and also because of the Gypsy camp that's close by. They were seated on the sand and looked out toward the open sea. When I got closer, they turned around.

"Hello!" I said.

They all answered at once. "Hello!"

On my way back, half an hour later, they were no longer there. The ocean was turning black; night was coming on. Out of habit, I looked at the house. I noticed a human shape disappearing rapidly around a corner. Well, well . . . Instead of checking on things straightaway, I made a detour and hid behind the neighboring house to watch. The six little Gypsies from the beach were there, playing a strange game. That is, of course, if you consider throwing a kid onto the roof of a house a game.

Because that's what they were doing! It took me a while before I could believe my eyes. It wasn't a cat or a dog they were throwing up; it was a real kid! The two taller ones grabbed him by his legs and arms, swung him three or four times, then threw him up just as you would a sack of potatoes. The little one hurtled into the air and landed right on the edge of the roof. He tried to grab the gutter but didn't make it and fell down. One of the kids dove and caught him in his arms just like in football. None of them laughed, which seemed odd. They talked for a moment and made a second attempt. But the same thing happened. The kid slid and fell down. This time they argued. No doubt the little kid had hurt himself. Two new throwers moved in. They wore caps with earflaps. They sent the kid into the air with unbelievable energy. I almost shouted for them to stop but it was too late. The kid went up so high that he almost reached the center of the roof. He hung on to it as if he were a large insect. Then he crawled toward the chimney. And down he went into it. . . .

Two minutes later, the garage door opened. They all rushed in. The door closed again. There was nothing more to see. I had watched, completely fascinated, and done nothing. I should have intervened, but I'm no Zorro. And I'm not paid a hundred dollars a month to have my stomach gutted. These Gypsies carry knives, we all know that. My job was to inform Faivre if something wasn't "in order." That's all. So I ran home and called him at his residence in Bordeaux.

"Mr. Faivre?"

"Speaking."

"It's Thierry Viard. I hope I'm not disturbing you?"

I told him exactly what I had witnessed. He listened silently. Then he asked only one question:

"They're Gypsies, you say?"

I wasn't one hundred percent sure but I said they were very likely Gypsies. He told me to keep an eye on the house in case they came out and that he was on the way. That he would be quick and would reward me for notifying him. And not to call the police. I put two parkas on top of each other and went back to the house. Nothing had changed. I waited by the road. Faivre arrived less than thirty minutes later. He must have barreled down the highway the whole trip. He stopped his car at a short distance so as not to make noise and walked toward me.

"Are they still inside?" he wanted to know.

"Yeah, I think they are."

"Well, then I need your help. Are you handy?"

There was a kind of exultation in his voice. It scared me. We took a flashlight, a wireless electric drill, and a toolbox from the trunk of his car.

"Come on."

We walked to the garage.

"Do you know how to attach the door to the ground so that it can't be opened?"

I stared at him in disbelief. "You want—"

"Do you know how?"

I nodded and got to work. In the meantime, Faivre went into the garage for a few seconds and came out with a handful of fuses. I drilled a hole into the concrete ground and screwed in a strong hook. I drilled another hole at the bottom of the metal garage door and also attached a hook. I joined the two hooks with a strong wire. It was a messy job but it was sturdy. Faivre tried to lift the door and it held. He winked at me and counted out four hundred-dollar bills. Good thing the front door could only be entered and exited with a key.

"For your trouble," he said. "Don't say anything to anybody. I'll be back in a week and I'll give you the same amount. Until then, do nothing. I trust you completely, Thierry. Can I drop you somewhere?"

I live nearby, so I said no.

He left. I put the money in my pocket and walked home. In the middle of the night, I woke up. It occurred to me that I wasn't doing much with my life but I didn't feel that I deserved better. And I started to cry.

# thirteen

## ACCOUNT OF GILLES FAIVRE,
### FIFTY-TWO YEARS OLD, BUSINESSMAN

They accuse me of cruelty. I must be dreaming. These people came into my house uninvited, but I guess that's irrelevant. Others would have resented it and gotten mad. Not me. I figured that these young people wanted to come in (and wanted to badly, since they engaged in a perilous stunt, as you know). So fine. Since it was their wish, it would have been inhospitable to prevent them from doing so, right? That's why I did nothing to make them leave. On the contrary, I made sure they took full advantage of their visit.

Nevertheless, I'm told my visitors stayed three days without food, without light, and that it was cold. I don't disagree. As a sign of repentance, I'm not exacting any rent from these visitors. Consider it a gift. And yet they say I'm heartless!

I was threatened with a court date, where I would have to apologize, and might even be brought up on charges. After all, it would only be fair. But these people sneaked into my house, damaged my furniture, dirtied my rugs. It's unforgivable, so of course I have to be punished, right? As for them, they're free to do as they please. Maybe they're breaking into another house at this very moment. Into your house maybe, and why not?

So it goes in this country. It's more honorable to steal from your neighbor than to make an honest living. That's just the way it is. But this is going to change sooner than anyone thinks. Some of us are hard at work on it. And our numbers are growing.

# fourteen

ACCOUNT OF RÉMY DOUTRELEAU,
FOURTEEN YEARS OLD, YANN'S BROTHER

When Yann opened the garage door, I rushed over to him.

"Bravo, Yann! Bravo!" I yelled, sweeping him into my arms.

He was covered with soot, his elbows and knees all scratched. He mimed for us the way he'd gone down the flue, the way mountain climbers do. We closed the door quickly and went to look for the fuse box to make light. Paul found it.

We removed our shoes to enter the living room. We didn't dare speak. The floor was covered with a huge rug like the ones you see in catalogs. In the middle was a low glass table, and around it were leather armchairs, each large enough to seat three people. Like a flock of birds, we went from room to room. There were at least five bedrooms, all of them tidy and clean.

"These are girls' rooms," Pierre said.

He was right. Only girls spread knickknacks on shelves and hang posters of celebrities on walls. Later, in the living room, we found proof: a framed photo of seven girls, with their parents. Very pretty girls, all blond and graceful, just like their mother. The father was beaming a wide smile in the picture. He seemed like a nice guy. We said we wouldn't damage anything and that we'd leave a note of apology before leaving the next day.

In the kitchen, the refrigerator was empty. Same for the cabinets, except for a pack of crackers that we immediately shared. We took some blankets from the girls' beds and put them on the rug in the living room. No use dirtying the bedrooms. We'd all sleep together and keep each other warm.

"Is there a TV?" Victor asked.

There wasn't, so Paul turned on the CD player. We told him not to, but when he gets something in his head. . . . The music was sad and we eventually turned it off. Yet strangely, it also pleased me. I looked at the CD case. The piece was called "Suite for Cello" and the composer was Bach. Some people listen to bizarre things.

"What about opening the shutters?" Max suggested. "Maybe we'll see the ocean from here?"

Suddenly the light went off. A few seconds later, we heard the noise of an electric drill.

# fifteen

If at least we'd had a watch! We'd have known whether it was day or night! In the dark, it was all the same. In spite of all the blankets in the house, the little ones were coughing nonstop. From time to time, Paul and I went to the garage and kicked the door as hard as we could and swore all we could. It didn't help but we felt better.

Unable to see, we became like blind people: we felt with our hands.

The worst was to think that the ocean was right in front of us, maybe one hundred yards away, and that we couldn't look at it! We were like sardines in a tin can. Impossible to open the shutters since the electricity had gone out and impossible to open the garage door. I knocked on it hard with Pierre! I even stubbed the big toe of my left foot.

Being on the beach was the best time of my life. We sat together, and as the sun set, the water took on a steel color. We felt very small, but also protected. The ocean made a lot of noise. I can't describe it.

There was no one around. Only this guy with a

hat on his head who ran by us. He said hello and we answered the same.

I wasn't too worried; I knew we'd get out of there. I didn't know how, but we would get out.

## Rémy's Account

In the middle of the night (if it was night actually), Victor whispered in the deep silence:

"It's our birthday."

It was true. He and Max had turned twelve. So we hugged them and gave them kisses. We started to sing "Happy Birthday" but were too sad to finish the song.

We were all thirsty. That was the worst.

## Max's Account

Victor and I stayed under the blankets 'cause we'd caught cold. To kill time at the beginning, we played animal riddles. Then we stopped playing. We wanted to go back home. Victor coughed so much that he threw up on the rug. "They're going to scold me. They're going to scold me," he kept saying. Fabien told him not to worry, not to cry about that.

## Victor's Account

Max and I had a fever and stayed under the blankets. I threw up on the rug, but it wasn't important. I didn't cry about that. I had weird dreams of us walking along the railroad track, with the father leading us. "Come on," he said. "We're going to the ocean! You know the way!" And he laughed. I didn't like that dream.

## Rémy's Account

Paul found a lighter in a drawer, but the flame was very small and it burned our fingers. With the light, we looked at the photo of the seven girls and their parents. They kept smiling. . . . In a rage, I threw it as hard as I could and I think I broke a lamp.

## Pierre's Account

It suddenly occurred to me that if we couldn't get heat from the radiators, there was the fireplace! Why not make a fire! I shared my idea with Paul and he agreed. All the pieces of furniture were a good source of wood. We went into one of the bedrooms and tore apart a bed. Not an easy job when you can't see a thing. We were unable to break the planks and we would have had to push them little by little into the fire. Since there was no newspaper to light the blaze, we tore pages from the first large book we put our hands on. But our fire never got started. We only succeeded in creating a lot of smoke and couldn't open any windows to let fresh air in.

## FABIEN'S ACCOUNT

I no longer knew whether we had been here two days or one week. Everything was mixed up in my mind. I remember there was a moment when no one was moving, and for the first time I thought maybe we were going to die here together. Would it be painful or would we go to sleep quietly? Who would go first? And who last? I was asking myself these questions when Yann came over and scratched my arm.

"What's the matter?" I asked him.

He took my hand and put the very thing we had been looking for from the beginning in it. We had searched every room, every nook and crack, even under the kitchen sink.

"Let's give up. There isn't one around," I had said.

It was a telephone!

I took the lighter and lit it close to Yann's face.

"Where did you find it?" I asked him in a whisper.

*In a cardboard box, on top of the dresser, in the parents' bedroom.*

"Then we're saved?"

*Yes, you're saved.*

The lighter went off. I managed to light it again one last time. Yann's smiling face seemed to dance in the glimmer of the flame and then disappeared in the dark. It was the last time I saw him. But I did not know. Now, when I think of him, I always see his smiling face dancing in the light and hear him telling me, *You're saved.*

We still had to find the jack, which turned out to be really difficult. At the beginning, we looked feverishly, all of us on all fours, even Victor and Max. After what seemed like hours, we got discouraged. All except for Paul.

"It's got to be behind a piece of furniture!" he said.

So we moved all the pieces of furniture that were against the walls. We were perspiring. We were out

172

of breath. We stank. We bumped into each other in the dark. We were like animals. Finally, the only piece of furniture left was a huge trunk in the hallway. Gathering our last bit of energy, we pushed it away. Paul followed the baseboard with his fingers.

"I've got it," he said very quietly, no longer having the strength to shout. "I've got the jack."

Rémy fetched the phone from the living room and we were able to connect it. We all held our breath. In the silence, the dial tone sounded faint and frail, but it was as if ten windows of the house had opened at once, as if the ocean had burst through them!

"Who do we call?" Pierre asked once we regained our calm.

It was an important question. The police would take us back home. A random number, well, what would we say to a stranger? We couldn't even say where we were, except that it was a house near the ocean and that they all looked alike. And how do you even dial a number when you can't see a thing?

Silence again. Suddenly we heard the *beep, beep, beep* of the touch phone. I extended my arm to grope around and found Yann's hand. He was dialing a number. After the tenth *beep*, he gripped my arm very tightly and handed me the phone. I brought it to my ear.

It rang twice; then I heard our mother's voice.

"Hello? Who's this?"

"It's us," I said crying. "It's us."

All the others started crying too, except for Pierre, who shouted, "Shut up!" because he wanted to hear.

"Where are you, children?" she asked. I had never heard her call us children before.

"We're locked up in a house, near the ocean."

"Shut up!" she shouted, but it wasn't meant for us. She was shouting at Corniaud, who was barking near her.

We all started laughing.

"Do you hear? It's Corniaud! It's Corniaud!" I said.

Then our father spoke to us. Paul repeated that we were locked up in a house, and he explained the road we had taken with the fat grocer, how far the house was and all that. The father said that he was calling the Bordeaux police and that he and the mother would be here before dawn, not to worry. He too called us children, which seemed equally strange.

Before dawn? Was it nighttime still then?

We hung up the phone and scooted back under the blankets in the living room. It was terribly cold. We huddled against each other and went to sleep.

# sixteen

ACCOUNT OF XAVIER CHAPUIS,
FORTY-TWO YEARS OLD, POLICE SERGEANT MAJOR

The Doutreleau case? I have to concede that I had given up on it. When a child disappears and is not found within forty-eight hours, it doesn't look promising. The more time passes, the less chance of success. Days go by, weeks, and you end up forgetting or almost forgetting until, one day, a mushroom picker finds a corpse in the woods. In this case, it had been five full days, and just as many nights. Of course, we searched. The police over in the Doutreleaus' town had brought in dogs early on, but the rain had washed away all traces. Then they flew over the area in a helicopter. Nothing. And yet seven kids on the loose had to be noticeable! Later we learned they took a train!

I'm the one who answered the radio call during the night of Saturday to Sunday. The father Doutreleau had received a phone call from his children: they were in a house by the ocean, close by. He described the road, so I had an idea. And he indicated that a fat grocer had taken them there. When you say "a fat grocer" in this area, people automatically answer in unison: Ducroq! Four of us hustled to wake up Ducroq and he led us straight to the house. The problem was that I knew the house in question— I knew who it belonged to. It belonged to Faivre, if you see who I mean? We tried to reach him at his main residence but got no answer. So we entered through the garage door, which, strangely enough, was locked from the outside with a wire.

If you're familiar with the painting *The Raft of the Medusa*, you'll understand the scene that our flashlights lit up. The kids were in a total state of lethargy. In a daze. And weak. A strong smell of vomit and urine permeated the room. It was also very cold inside. All the kids were lying on the floor, tangled up in blankets, dirty and thin. The light blinded them. We turned our flashlights away.

"It's okay, kids. Everything will be fine," I said.

"Do you have something to drink?" one of them, the taller one, asked.

His lips were swollen. I went to the kitchen, but the tap was dry. We immediately called for ambulances, requesting that they bring water.

179

I don't know how we let the smaller one escape. I guess we weren't vigilant enough. He probably slipped through the open garage door. By the time we noticed, it was too late. We searched for him all night and all the next day. It's still the greatest mystery for me. If he had walked toward the beach and drowned, the ocean would have brought his body back. And if he had stayed on earth, I swear we would have found him. I don't know what became of the little guy. That's the only answer I can give when I'm asked: I don't know.

But I do know that some of his brothers gave us hell when they had to board the ambulance without him. The two older twins were reasonable.

"We'll find him, don't worry," I told them.

They trusted me. The smaller twins were no longer conscious. According to a paramedic, they were running a high fever and were motionless when they were placed on the stretchers.

However, the middle twins rebelled. The poor kids just wouldn't listen to reason. Their legs were wobbly, yet they ran toward the ocean.

"Yann! Yann!" they screamed.

And they put up a fight. When their ambulance drove away, the one who had twisted my thumb was still hitting the rear door.

"He can't swim! He can't swim!" he kept crying out.

# seventeen

My name is Yann Doutreleau. I am ten years old.

On a very rainy November night, I convinced my brothers to flee our parents' farm. We went west. My brothers were caught five days later near Bordeaux, at a place by the ocean.

That night was not of my choice. . . .

I wasn't sleeping. I was huddled against Fabien; I could feel his warmth and regular breath against my cheek. In spite of the rain spattering, I heard voices downstairs. Usually, the parents slept at night. They fought only in the daytime. So I went down to listen. The bed creaked a little. Fabien asked me where I was going. I told him.

With my ear pressed against the door of our parents' room, I learned nothing new. Only that they had no money left. That the mother was going to ask for assistance. That lots of people did. The father objected. He preferred to die. And for all of us to die with him.

The rain came down heavier still. They grew silent. Then, after a while, the mother asked:

"What about them cats?"

I shuddered. I hadn't thought they knew. Our cat had given birth to seven kittens the day before. I was there when they came out of their mother's tummy. I had seen her lie down, meow three times in pain and push. She scratched at the straw. The kittens were born under my eyes, all seven of them. She licked them from head to tail, until each kitten was clean, dry and warm. Then she lay down over them, giving one last meow.

*Well done, kitty,* I told her.

Now the mother was repeating, "What about them cats?"

"I'll kill the seven of 'em tomorrow mornin'," the father answered.

Rage filled my heart. Filled my entire body. I felt it in my hands, my shoulders. I became a block of rage. I went back upstairs and tugged on the sleeve of Fabien's sweater.

*We have to leave, Fabien! Quick! All of us! Before dawn!*

He wanted to know why, so I told him our parents wanted to do us . . . harm.

We woke up our brothers, and after dressing as warmly as possible, out we went into the night. It didn't take long before we were drenched, frozen . . . and lost.

I was walking in front. Fabien and Rémy were close behind. Our other brothers followed, holding hands. The youngest ones were whining.

---

When the police opened the garage door, I slipped outside and waited for the ambulances to arrive. I hid in the first one, under the passenger seat, and did not move. Later, as the ambulance was on its way to Bordeaux, I saw Rémy's hand hanging from the stretcher. I held out my arm and tickled his palm with my nails. He crawled up a bit to see who

186

it was. His eyes went wide. I just had time to put my finger across my lips.

*Rémy, listen to me. I've something important to tell you. Our parents did not want to kill us. It's only the cats they wanted to kill. You understand? You'll tell the others, won't you?*

He nodded. We held hands until we reached Bordeaux. I let go only when the ambulance stopped at the hospital.

*You'll tell the others, won't you?* I said again.

I waited until everyone had gone before coming out of my hiding spot. The town was deserted and cold. I threw a blanket that I had found in the ambulance over my shoulders, a brown blanket that I wore like a cape.

# eighteen

ACCOUNT OF JEAN MARTINIÈRE,
SIXTY YEARS OLD, SKIPPER, MERCHANT MARINE

A little boy was seated Indian-style on the deck of the ship. A brown blanket covered his shoulders. We had left the port of Bordeaux in the morning with grain in the hold. I only carry merchandise in my freighter, no passengers.

"Hey, you, what are you doing here?" I asked.

The child did not seem bothered by my question. He looked at me over his shoulder and smiled the most beautiful smile. The kind of smile that cuts your anger short. I'm a grandfather and a child like this one can turn me to putty.

"Have you lost your tongue? Where do you expect to go? Where were you hiding?"

No answer. And always that smile. It was very strange. I had the sudden impression that this child wasn't real, that he had stepped right out of a fairy tale. That he was granting me the right to enter the tale for a moment. That he was willing to take me in. Of course, I had to stop asking stupid questions.

Gingerly, I sat next to him, taking care not to destroy the magic. It was incredibly mild for a mid-November morning. Above us, the sky was immense. The ship was moving at a good speed.

Due west.

**ABOUT THE AUTHOR**

**JEAN-CLAUDE MOURLEVAT** taught German for many years before devoting himself to the theater as an actor, teacher, and director. He then began writing for young people and has become a prolific and beloved author of children's books in his native France, where his novels have garnered numerous literary awards. *The Pull of the Ocean* (titled *L'enfant Océan* in French) won France's prestigious Prix Sorcières.